Joseph Hudson Young

Lyrics. Fjelda - The Great Bridge, in the Happy Summer Time, etc.

Joseph Hudson Young

Lyrics. Fjelda - The Great Bridge, in the Happy Summer Time, etc.

ISBN/EAN: 9783744788472

Printed in Europe, USA, Canada, Australia, Japan

Cover: Foto ©Andreas Hilbeck / pixelio.de

More available books at **www.hansebooks.com**

FJELDA, THE GREAT BRIDGE, IN THE HAPPY SUMMER TIME, ETC.

Thou who stealest fire
From the fountains of the past
To glorify the present,— * * * *
* * * * * * * * *
My friend, with thee to live alone
Were how much better than to own
A crown, a scepter and a throne!
—*Tennyson.*

BY

JOSEPH HUDSON YOUNG.

————— —— —————

FUNK & WAGNALLS
NEW YORK: LONDON:
1889
18 AND 20 ASTOR PLACE.   44 FLEET STREET.

FUNK & WAGNALLS,
18 and 20 Astor Place,
NEW YORK.

CONTENTS.

		PAGE
THE GREAT BRIDGE,	. . . . . .	5
THE ARCTIC HEROES, .	. .	10
THE STORM,	. . . . . .	. 12
THE AUGURY,	. . .	. 13
BEYOND,	. . . .	15
A DEAD LOVE,	.	17
AMOR CREATOR DEUS,		19
HOPE,	. . .	22
BEREFT,	. . .	. 23
CAN I FORGET,		25
JANUARY,	.	27
FEBRUARY,	.	28
MARCH,	.	. 29
APRIL,	.	30
MAY,	. .	. 31
JUNE,	.	32
JULY,	.	. 33
AUGUST,		34
SEPTEMBER,	. . .	. 35
OCTOBER,	. .	36
NOVEMBER,	. .	. 37
DECEMBER,	. . . .	38
ATHANASIA,	. . .	. 39
HERO'S LAMENT,	. .	40
ORION,	. .	. 43

CONTENTS.

	PAGE
My Ship Come In,	46
A Reverie,	48
In the Happy Summer Time,	52
Remembrance,	55
Ode IV., Book I., Horace,	57
Ode VII., Book I., Horace,	59
Liberty,	61
Percy Bysshe Shelley,	66
Lilian Adelaide Neilson,	68
Westchester—Idyl,	70
Frederick III.,	77
Harry Brandon,	78
Edward M'Glynn,	79
The Miserly Millionaire,	80
Spring,	81
The New and Vulgar Rich,	82
Miss Clara St. Clair and Her Millionaire,	85
The Mescal of Montezuma,	89
Toung Taloung,	93
My Lover True,	96
Love's Anchorite,	98
The Poet and the Bird,	100
Forever and Forever,	102
"No,"	104
The Autumn Flight,	106
Fjelda,	110
The Maid of Rome,	114
The Wreck,	124

INVOCATION.

T O whom, to whom
Shall my hand inscribe this book ?
To the spirit of the brook,
Of the brook that ever goeth ;
To the spirit of the wind,
Of the wind that bloweth, bloweth ;
To the spirit of the sea,
Of the sea that ever floweth ;
To ye, yes, to ye,
Ye earth-encircling three ;
To these, ay, to these—
The rivers, winds and seas,
Will the poet's hand inscribe the poet's book.
Blow it, blow it everywhere,
Breezes of the boundless air ;
Rills and rivers, bear it on,
From the country to the town,
From the city back again—
My book, oh, bear it, rills and rivers,
To and fro, until it quivers,
Flying, like a weaver's shuttle, through the minds of men.

And thou, O mighty sea,
　Still bear it back to me;
The poet's bread upon thy waters thrown—
　Oh, give him back his own.

　　O loyal friend! O true
　　And tender sweetheart, you,
O heart, forever loyal, true, and tender!
The poet's heart of hearts is only thine,
Round which his love's full-clustering passion-vine,
Purple and green, doth creep and cling and twine.
　　Wherever thou dost bide,
　　The river, wind and tide
Shall tell thee this: that, in the gathering gloom,
O loyal friend, O sweetheart true and tender,
　　The poet's thought
　　With thee is fraught;
His darkness lighted with thy soft eyes' splendor;
While round thy head, one with thy radiant hair,
　　Like the bright star, Altair,
　　Shineth the aureole
　　Of a sweet, childlike soul.

THE GREAT BRIDGE.

WRITTEN FOR THE OPENING DAY

HEN Earth was young,
    The breasts she offered to her human child,
    Deserts of chaos, floods and forests wild
      Were hid among.
    A foundling flung
    From mystery
    To history,—
    A wanderer fate-impelled,
    Her savage heart rebelled
    To own the hapless thing
    Of dust and ashes. Sing,
Ye Muses nine, whose forms seraphic stand
Luminous on the far, horizon land
Of setting ages, in the twilight dim
Of fading eras, sing, ay, sing of him—
    Creation's slave and conquering lord.
    A newer song than arms afford
Those deeds inspire, which, in the march of mind,
Crossing wide seas vast wildernesses find,
And leave a monumental world behind.

Clio, thy sounding lyre
Too long has found an echo where the wings
Of ruin-haunting creatures stir the air
That vibrates to the music of thy strings,-
    Ravens and vampires dire.
And thou, Eolus, let thy thunders deep,
That in the striving elements resound,
Subside into the gentle tones that sweep
The silken harp, a harmony profound.
For here the Angel of good-will to men
And all the arts of peace has strung for thee
A nobler harp than any yet whose strain
Has given back the ocean's minstrelsy,
        When breezes fair
        Press the white sail,
        And every gale
        Coursing the air
Compels the wandering ships into a fleet.
As the sure collie gathers, one by one,
The snowy sheep, and, with the setting sun,
Follows them home—the ewes with swelling teat,
The horned ram, and lambs that leaping run.
So, to the music of this lute of thine,
Eolus, shepherd of the plains of brine,
The ships shall gather, flocking in the Gate; —
Huge merchantmen weighed down with goodly freight,

The bristling frigate, and the squadron gay
That skims the wave and dances on the bay.
  O Bridge, whose towers
  Prophetic stand,
  To show the land
  Her silent powers !
 The multitudinous flow
 Of tides, that come and go,
All noiseless moves below thy heaving hight;
 Above, with murmuring tread,
 The living and the dead
Together pass, to rest them for the night.
  O glorious span !
  Triumphal arch !
  No chieftain's march,
  No rat-a-plan
 Of drums, victorious from the fray,
 Inaugurates this happier day.
Two cities populous now consummate
 Their vow to be as one.
Imperial union ! The imperial State
 Ascends a worthy throne.
Almighty Builder, interweave each strand
 With hope and confidence.
So stretch the giant cords throughout the land,
 Our strength and our defence.

Upheld by truth and justice' massive towers,
    The way shall lie secure
To peace and liberty, whose happy hours
    Unbroken shall endure.

      I stand below
      The Eastern tower.
      The midnight hour,
      Supreme and slow,
Issues from out the groaning throat of Time.
Oppressed beneath Eternity, his soul
Utters in yonder tongue of iron its dole
Of weariness and woe.   The cry sublime
Pervades the night, while to the stars it calls,—
The watchmen on the far eternal walls,—
      " What of the night? "
They seem to pause a moment—Hercules,
Whose labors crown him one among the gods;—
On mountains piled he reached those bright abodes ;
Such power has toil the thrones of heaven to seize.—
And great Orion, ancient pioneers,
To answer from their constellated spheres—
      " 'Twas all in vain,
      " Their labor, when
      " The sons of men,
      " From Babel's plain,

" On stairways imminent
"Did climb the firmanent.
" But now the gods, themselves confounded, see
" Them walk a causeway laid upon the skies.
" They shall to more heroic honors rise,—
"Span thought's wide gulf and give the soul her liberty."

THE ARCTIC HEROES.

OWARD no earthly pole their course is set;
  No earthly coast their faithful watch descries.
But that all undiscovered bourne, as yet,
  Salutes their wistful eyes.

The good Jeannette, she did not reach her goal;
  But, where she sank, her sister ship sailed on—
That spirit-craft, whose compass points the soul
  To shores beyond the Sun.

Her name is Destiny; and God's own hand
  Upon her helm by day and night is set.
The other sank, but this will make the land.
  She sank—the brave Jeannette.

The frightful Hydra coiled about the North,
  Whose hues with glittering scales of ice are blent,
Crushing, devoured her, while its breath went forth
  Freezing a continent.

But, those—the heroes, by some instinct mute
  Distinguishing the master from the prey,
It spared, and sent them on,—the watery brute—
  On their prophetic way.

10

Soothed by the subtle, life-expelling chill,
   There have been who have perished while they slept
Unmindful of the spell that bound their will
   And round their heart-strings crept.

If only this had been the blissful rest
   To their great labors! So, the Arctic snows
Had couched them on that frozen ocean's breast,
   And hushed in sleep their woes.

It was not written thus. The age has need
   Of sufferers whose truth shall exorcise
Man's noble soul of the ignoble greed
   That throttles it with lies,—

That weighs all values in those scales of strife,
   Whose standard is the pocket's sordid gain,—
That coins the moments of a brother's life,
   And worships the profane.

Oft as the Northern morning lights the far,
   Illimitable reaches of that arch
Whose glorious span o'ercanopies the star
   That led them on their march,

Our gazing thoughts in reverence will turn,
   As to a temple consecrated, fair,
Whose crystal piles are sculptures, that inurn
   Their fame who perished there.

THE STORM.

O, yonder, borne upon the treacherous flood
  A beauteous creature moves.
Were it a living soul, of flesh and blood,
  Fondly impelled by love's
Impetuous eagerness, it could not keep
A surer course ; it could not glide and sweep
In fairer, swifter flight across the deep.

But, look again ! Caught 'twixt the tempest's blast
  And madly surging seas,
The shattered sails beat helplessly ; and fast
  The fierce Eumenides,
Riding the winds, pursue the hapless thing.
Storm-lashed and driven, wave-swept and foundering,
Shoreward it drifts, a bird with broken wing.

It is thyself, my soul, upon that ocean
  Where the storm-spirit broods
Of passion and unrest and rapt emotion ;
  Swept by whose mighty moods,—
Up-borne to heaven, or downward hurled from sight,
Shoreward thou driftest, where the starless Night
Will find thee lying, still and cold and white.

THE AUGURY.

HE white sea-gulls float up from the bay;
  And their wings are wet with the salt sea
    dew.
Oh, what do the notes from their white throats
    say?
"Tidings, O watching-worn maiden, for you!"

The white sea-gulls float up from the bay;
  And their breasts are wet with the salt sea-dew.
Oh, what do the notes from their white throats say?
  "A spirit has flown to the shoreless blue."

When night and storm were out on the deep,
  And the birds of ocean slept on the wave,
A cry of despair broke across their sleep—
  "Lost, lost, my Father! Oh, hear me, and save"

And then the breaking clouds fled away;
  And a star shone out, of a light divine.
Uncoffined, unseen, in the dark green bay
  He lieth, embalmed in a shroud of brine.

13

He lieth ? No: only the form lies there ;–
  He liveth and loveth beyond the sun.
Nor has he forgotten the fond spot, where
  On earth the loved and the lover were one.

The white sea-gulls float up from the bay ;
  And their wings are wet with the salt sea-dew.
Oh, what do the notes from their white throats say ?
  " He liveth and loveth where all are true."

BEYOND.

GOLDEN Sun, sink down to rest
In the roseate arms of the azure West!
To-day, I swear, thou hast not seen
Or a field more fair, or a vale more green,
Than the vale and the field where my heart has been.

O shades of Evening, swiftly creep
O'er the arches sprung in the star-lit deep!
Ye will not reach a point more far,—
Ye will not unfold a diviner star
Than the sphere where my hopes and longings are.

O Moon, of searching eye profound!
In thy yearly course or thy monthly round,
Thou hast not found in earth a cave,
On her mountain slopes or below the wave,
Or more silent or dark than my love's deep grave.

O Night, of the lone, voiceless hour,
When the budding thought blooms a dreamy flower!
Thy visions have not filled my brain
With less empty themes, or a joy less vain
Than thy shadows that mantle the troubled main.

O Morning, bright and pure thou art
As the dawning love of an angel's heart,
More beaming, more serene the ray
That shall usher in the eternal day,—
That shall banish the night-shade of Earth away.

For oh, the field and vale lie where
They are fanned by gales of celestial air!
The sphere is immortality;
The grave—the past; mirth the fantasy,
And the morning—the dawn of the life for aye.

A DEAD LOVE.

HAT shall I do with my dead, dead love?
Cold on my heart it lies.
I cannot bury this dear, dead love
Forever from my eyes.

My love in life was pure and sweet,
Tender and true and strong.
I wept for joy to see the face
That I had loved so long.

Out of the West, the far Northwest,
At sunset all a-flame,—
Out of the dark, dark night, that follows,
After a year he came,

Into the night of my lonely life ;—
It was a glorious morn.
Ah, me! It was the saddest morrow,
Since he and I were born.

Is this thy hand, so cold, my darling,
That was so fond and free?
Are these thine eyes, so vacant,
That look, but do not see ?

My love in life was pure and sweet,
  Tender and true and strong.
I wept for joy to see the face
  That I had loved so long.

And not regret, nor mortal ruth
  Shall change the spirit, now,
Of the love, in life so true and tender,
  Dead of a broken vow.

AMOR CREATOR DEUS.

A FRAGMENT.

Love, when wert thou born,
  Child ever fair and young, though oft for-
    lorn,
  In passion's tatters clad,
In this so sad,
Unheavenly world of tears?
Eternal, sempiternal are thy years.
Necessity infinite thee begot,
The first, when all beside thyself was not,—
Thyself, the source and Sire of all that are,
The lowest atom and the highest star;
The faintest instinct, and the matchless eye
Of reason and the soul's authority.

O Love, when thou wert born,
The ethereal crystalline irradiate
With thy fair excellence
And gladness, whence
Glory supernal sprang,
Did mirror thee into thyself, and hang
The hight and depth with re-create portraitures

Of thy exquisite frontal. Who endures—
What soul, what sense howe'er divine, the sight
Of love to Love disclosed in its own light?
Blushing a thousand crimsons, through the vault
Of heaven, to veil thee from its fond default,
Thy face shot lightning, and it fell on fire,—
On chaos fell and conflagration dire.

O Love, O wondrous Love,
Within that hell of elements that strove,—
Within that lurid Night
Deep laid, thy white,
Innocent spirit slept
Serene and imperturbable, and kept
Its purpose sure in dreams that laid their spell
Of law and life upon the fire-mist's hell,—
In dreams, while æons came and went, that wove
Systems and suns throughout the nebulous Jove;
Thy purpose sure pushing its steadfast way
Through phantasms wild up to the primal day;
Through monads, through creations dumb it ran,
Of ox-eyed monsters, up to mind and man.

O Love, beautiful Love,
Upon that verge of super-sensuous sense
Thy dreaming footstep paused
In wonder, caused

By the pre-natal hour,
Full to the unfolding of the human flower
Consummate, sense and spirit, folded deep .
Within the blissful heart of Love asleep.
Inwardly stirred, that moment Love awoke,—
Awoke and slept again.   Then fell the stroke,
The first of Time recorded.   'T was the birth
Of love in Love's own image on the Earth,—
The advent of Creation's soul and lord,
In Nature's flesh, on Nature's native sward.

HOPE.

Love, the day declines
Far down the fading zone!
Life's morning light no longer shines
For me, as once it shone.

O love, the day goes down
Behind the silent zone!
The life whose light the gloam turns brown,—
Its birds of song have flown.

O love, the day is gone!
Dark night involves the zone.
Life its last pillow sleeps upon,
Death's pillow cold, of stone.

O love, day breaks again
O'er the celestial zone!
In heaven life wakes, and takes again
Thy truth's eternal throne.

BEREFT.

WHICH way, beloved, which way in this maze
Of many feet have thy dear footsteps passed
O my love lost to me, I stand and gaze
Again to see thee where I saw thee last,
As voyagers wrecked, on some lone island cast,
Gaze sea-ward in despair! Thus I, where all
Life's surging sea is solitude to him
Whose breaking heart is tearful to the brim,
And heaven's departing day a mourner's pall
To eyes that thou dost not illuminate,
Thou shining lode-star of my passionate,
Tremulous soul.   Oh, hast thou set for aye?
Which way, beloved, in this maze which way?

Which way, beloved?   From the rythmic spheres
A sense has thrilled me, in the lonely hour
That, pausing, flies apace, as one who fears
Darkness and solitude,—the mystic hour
When spirits pass, and mortals feel their power.
It was thy step upon the bound of time.
Which way, beloved, through the whispering air?
Which way, beloved, on the heavenly stair

Invisible ascending?　O sublime
Above the apprehension of my sight
Ethereal, seraphic, in the Light
Of light rapt and withdrawn, thou art divine:
And my life lost shall find itself in thine.

CAN I FORGET.

CAN I forget?
   It thus may be, when years have told their
     tale,
   And left their frosty chaplets on my head,
   With a long lifetime's sorrows overlaid.
And I am bowed and pale,—
      But, oh, not yet.

     Nor then forget.
But if, alas, time's ever onward flight
Should, while it wastes the form, prey on the soul
And rust the springs of memory that unroll
The past; and all be night,—
      Then, but not yet.

     Nor then; for when
So fond, so loving fond, so passionate,
My heart recalls the moments we have passed,
So priceless dear, so sacred at the last—
Till death I'll not forget;
      Then—only then.

And oh, nor then!
For when is passed the cold and bridgeless river,
Shall not I clasp a seraph's form to me,
In whose rapt eye thy spirit's glance I see?
Never the Archer's quiver
     To fear again.

JANUARY.

 DASHING youth is he whose coursers fleet
　　Outrun the steeds of Phœbus' flying car.
　　His horses are the winds, his lash the sleet
　　He rides the storm, and cometh from afar,—
The world where everlasting ages are.
But he is young, and beautiful his feet
Upon the mountains of the morn.　We greet,
O happy Year and New, we greet thy face
　　And hail in thee fond hope's eternal star.
Be thou propitious, and thy dwelling place
　　For aye shall be our hearts, nor memory mar
　　Thy feature's fair with rue's regretful scar.—
But look, look there! a shade—a spectre fast
Behind him rides.　Alack! my heart, it is the past.

27

FEBRUARY.

THE darkness deepens just before the day,
When night on night sweeps downward
from the pole.
Then watchers weary for the morning pray,
The noisome dews exhale, as it they stole
From yawning sepulchres. Upon my soul,
O Winter, now at length thy shadows lay,
As if the weeks would never wear away;
And dank and grewsome is thy feverous breath.
Hark! Wailing bells—heavy and hoarse; they toll.
Timing their measures to the march of death.
Be still, sad heart: the waves of grief that roll
Tremendous o'er thy sinking hopes,—their goal
Is Elys' happy shore, and they shall bear
Thy sorrow on their crest, and lay it safely there.

MARCH.

A, wild and wayward offspring of the Sun!
   First-born from his reunion with the sphere
   That turns again to greet his kiss upon
   The inconstant face, which shuns him every
       year,
And every year repents 'mid the severe
Regrets and penances of winter dun,
Drear, dark, and desolate;—the frigid nun
Among her sister planets. Headstrong child,
   Thou wouldst despoil the hopes, that now appear
In greening blades and swelling buds, beguiled
   By thee, thou counterfeit, whose treacherous leer
   Takes on a smile. For when subsides her fear
And Life from long duress adventures forth—
Full in her face thy blast hurls havoc from the North.

29

APRIL.

O SEASON, throned above the Pleiades,
    That, setting, weep afresh to see thee rise
    Supremely regent o'er the rainy seas
        Aerial, which issue from their eyes;—
Thy robe of purple is the rainbow's dyes,
All spangled with the fleck of golden bees
Early astir among the maple trees.
Nor is she less a woman than a queen,
    Who changes with her shifting mind the skies;
So varying moods diversify the scene,—
    Or cold, or warm, or gay, or full of sighs,
    As now she, beaming, laughs or, frowning cries,—
Eager to make and passionate to mar
The joy of Spring, wherein she shines the morning star.

30

MAY.

THE apple-blossoms of the sweet month of May
Upon the maiden Spring's uplifted brow
Fall, in a bridal veil of balmy spray.
She seeks from Heaven annunciation now :
It is her wedding-day; and He, whose vow
Forever, with an everlasting " Yea,"
Swears that the seed-time shall not pass away,—
He is the bridegroom,—Faith and Nature's God.
O happy bride, whom Love does thus endow
With bliss deific, thrilling deep the sod
That man has lacerated with his plow.
And then thy joy inspires all nature; thou
Dost come rejoicing, with a choiring train
Of mated birds, whose songs warble their love's refrain.

JUNE.

LOVE, the month, the day, the hour is here;
  And where art thou? Oh, come! my
   couch is spread
  Upon the immaculate bosom of the year
Throbbing with life, whose current, rich and red,
Breaks in the blush of roses that appear
When heaven tells its secret in her ear.
  And mine? Ah, listen!—roses for thy bed
Strewed thick and odorous, and lilies fair
  Massed in a pillow for thy fairer head—
Thy own sweet breath and thy own lustrous hair
  Shall shame them both. Oh, come! through arbors green
  And labyrinths of climbing eglantine—
Oh, come, my love! oh, haste! oh, fly to me!
In June I pant, I thirst, I faint, I die for thee.

32

JULY.

FORBEAR, O muse! I scarce can climb the
    ground
    Precipitous, uprising with the height
    Of great Olympus into depths profound.
There sits The Thunderer. Sharp lightnings light
The eyes that, under old Egypta's night
Draping his brows, flash forked fire. The sound
Falling strikes heavily, and with a bound
Reverberating peals along the sky.
    The ocean groans, rolling all ghastly white
And men and beasts and birds together fly.
    O boy, beware that tree. Dread Heaven! thy blight—
    Thy thunder-blight has struck, and in the sight—
The sight of his fond eyes its glare expires.
His name was Ganymed, and love the death-bolt fires.

33

AUGUST.

THE year is ripening; her girlhood's thrill
    Is growing fast into a matron's care.
      In clustering grapes the blood begins to
        fill,—
The smell of blooming corn-fields loads the air
With richness. Hear, O Heaven, a mother's prayer,
And gently lead her anxious feet, until
In Autumn's perfect joy thy blessed will
Be done. She hears; and Virgo intervenes,
    Blending her smile with Sol's too fervid glare.
Severely chaste she tempers it, and screens
    The panting Earth. But do thou still beware
    The dog-star's reign. Look skyward! Sirius there
Now rages, while he bays the rising moon—
The harvest moon, as soft as eve and fair as noon.

SEPTEMBER.

POMONA, goddess of the year, thy horn
  Is poured into the lap of Autumn crowned
The Queen of queens, laughing them all to
    scorn,
Such peace and joy within her realm abound.
Knee-deep the wallowing wheel goes gaily round
Crushing the juicy pulp. The full-ripe corn,
Of stalk and husk and silken tassel shorn,
Glitters in golden heaps that frequent lie,
  The shining ore of mines above the ground,—
Bringing to pass the early prophecy
  Of yellow daffodils. The love profound
  Of Nature's heart in man and brute is wound
In grateful ties about thine own, O God,
Incarnate, first and last, in the immortal clod.

OCTOBER.

STOOD alone, and Memory came near.
    Pensive she came, borne on the dreamy
      wings
    Of thoughts that fill the Autumn of the
year,
When Silence lays her hand upon the strings
Of Nature's harp, where Summer's echoings
Linger through ripe September.—Hark! The sere
And falling leaf. O Death! and art thou here
Concealed amid the shadows?—Pushing back
    Untimely Winter, warm October swings
The closing portals of the Zodiac
    Open again. The autumnal splendor flings
    On passing Summer and her precious things
A pall of glory. Thus, oh thus, my heart,
Will love transfigure death, when life and thou do part?

NOVEMBER.

ILGRIM of time, thy feet approach a land
　　Where all is desert,—bleak and mournful
　　shore,
　　Where leafless trees, for skeletons, upstand,
And dismal winds, for wailing ghosts, deplore;
The shore of a dead sea, encrusted o'er
With frozen dews.　Ah, me! the barren strand
Of age awaits us all, and the command,
Dreadful and stern, " Go forward."　On that brink,
　O Thou, in whom our Father we adore,
Divide the waters deathly cold, that shrink
　The soul with fear.　Yet now we live.　And more
　Wouldst thou?　Look back : the past was once before.
The cup within thy hand is Heaven's choice;
This, this alone, is sure ; oh, drink it and rejoice

DECEMBER.

A N old man, bent with age and reft of hope
    Plods heavily along a drifting road.
      'T is night. The tempest howls. In one
        fell swope
All ills together join to overload
The steps whose youth the whirlwind did forbode,—
Harvest of stormy seed. Look! on the slope
Verging the grave he totters. Cease to cope,
O single handed, with almighty Fate.—
    Alas! the old man reaps but that he sowed.
Resign thee, whose repentance comes too late.
    When he was young, from out their cold abode
    And cavernous, he loosed the winds, that showed
No mercy to the traveler, whose woes
Now overtake and leave him lost in his own snows.

ATHANASIA.

MORTAL, so fine and fragile is that thread
  Whereon thy life suspended hangs, no eye
 But One, whose vision keen hath numbered
  The sands of shores whose leagues un-
   measured lie,
Hath seen it; yet a whole eternity
Ineffable, in one quick moment dread,
Along its quivering tension may be sped.
Infinite soul, conjoined with finite clay,
 Thou art a star alight of God most High
His life thy being. Passing swift away
 The dust consumes, but thou shalt shine for aye;
 As light of stars accounted dead—shalt fly
On, on, and ever on, throughout the vast
Of thought,—forever present and forever past.

HERO'S LAMENT.

I.

Hero.

H! have you seen my boy—
My beautiful, blue-eyed boy?
Hither he swam—he swam to me;
Oh! save him from the dreadful sea.

Fishermen.

No, no, no,—we have not seen your boy,
Your beautiful, blue-eyed boy.

Hero.

Wo, wo, wo,—the light of life was in his eye.

Fishermen.

A light? Oh, yes; we saw a light,
Against the foaming face of night.
Flashing it died
Upon the tide.

Hero.

'T was love lit by despair—
It was his fond soul's prayer
Within his eye that burned so brilliantly.

All.

Wo, wo, wo,—my beautiful, beautiful boy
My beautiful, blue-eyed boy.

40

II.

Hero.

Oh! have you seen my boy—
My beautiful, blue-eyed boy?
Hither he swam—he swam to me,
Oh! save him from the stormy sea.

Fishermen.

No, no, no,—we have not seen your boy,
Your beautiful, blue-eyed boy.

Hero.

Wo, wo, wo,—the song of songs was in his voice.

Fishermen.

A song? Ah, yes; we heard a song
Upon the storm-wind borne along;
  It rose and fell,
  As when a bell,
Wondrously sweet and clear,
Rings in the sleeper's ear,
  Swung by some hand
  In fairy-land.

Hero.

'T was love against despair,
Braving the billows there;
He sang of me amid the tempest's noise.

All.

Wo, wo, wo,—my beautiful, beautiful boy,
My beautiful, blue-eyed boy.

III.

Hero.

Oh! have you seen my boy—
My beautiful, blue-eyed boy?
Hither he swam—he swam to me ;
Oh! save him from the raging sea.

Fishermen.

No, no, no,—we have not seen your boy,
Your beautiful, blue-eyed boy.

Hero.

Wo, wo, wo,—immortal youth was in his heart.

Fishermen.

Immortal? Ay, we saw a form—
A spirit soaring in the storm,
        God-like and free,
        . Glorious to see.
" Hero "—it called again,
And, beckoning, vanished then.

Hero.

.ın ! cruel fate, to rend our lives apart.

All.

Wo, wo, wo,—my beautiful, beautiful boy
My beautiful, blue-eyed boy.

ORION.

WHEN from her realm autumnal Summer flies,
And sceptered Winter rules the inverted
skies,—
As on the empyreal heights his throne he
takes,
Behold, to heaven the azure concave breaks
Clear as a crystal vault, whose arch appears
Resplendent with a myriad starry spheres,
Whose radiant legions from the East pursue
Orion, as he charges on, to view
The dread encounter while his arms engage
In god-like strife the Bull's terrific rage.
Upon his face three orbs inferior glow,
And round his head a seeming halo throw.
Each shoulder labors with a strength divine;
Here Bellatrix, there Betelguese shine,
As if the wrathful energies, that strove,
Shot fiery flashes in the face of Jove.
One sturdier arm a sturdy weapon bears,
With which the hero neither asks nor spares.
A lion's tawny hide the left adorns,
And challenges the Bull's defiant horns.

43

He stripped it from a royal monster slain
In the deep wilds of Themiscyra's plain,
When, by his mother taught, he chased and slew,
The mightiest hunter that the forest knew.
Three suns immense, in cosmic order placed,
Gleam in the girdle that surrounds his waist
And cheer the night-lorn wanderer at sea,
And guide his bark across the watery lea.
A falchion hangs obliquely by his side,
Its trusty blade in bloody crimson dyed,
And bright with stars that once were jewels set
In the queen-mother's golden coronet,—
Euryale, the Amazonian fair.
She charmed Posseidon from his ocean lair.
The god enraptured, sinking on her breast,
Her embryo son with race divine impressed.
Upon his ancle, of superior flame
Burns the imperial orb Rigel by name ;
As if he trod, so terrible his ire,
His way sublime in steps of living fire ;
And Saiph shines on his unbended knee.
A silver joint in the dun panoply.

Strive on, Orion, god-sprung hero, strive !
Thy name, a blazonry of stars, will live
When other names and fames forgotten sleep,
And Chaos laughs where Clio once did weep ;—

When mouldering monuments turn memory
Itself to dust; when sunken seas are dry,
And all the world a grave; when Earth's high noon
Wears the cold pallor of her long lost moon;—
When Earth herself, with all her tribes, lies drowned
In great Eternity's dread, fathomless profound.

MY SHIP COME IN

I BREATHED an atmosphere of love,—
　　'Twas life I long had sought,—
　Stirred by the pinions of a dove
　　That brooded o'er my thought.

I saw her first, that summer day
　When standing by the main,
Launching my fairy ship away.
　To the rich isles of Spain.

The wind, that shook the dreamy sail,
　Played with her tresses sweet;
And caught away her tangled veil,
　And laid it at my feet.

And when I gave it back to her,
　Her soft eyes spake to me;
And I was made a prisoner
　Chained by their modesty.

O isles of Spain!　O shores afar!
　What were your treasures now?
O'er life's wide sea a brighter star
　Rose on my tossing prow.

It led me to her side again;
  My thought was grown to love.
We launched our ship upon the main
  I and my household dove.

And, guided by that star, we steered
  Our course to the fair isle,
Where fortune's storms no more are feared,
  And pleasures ever smile.

A REVERIE.

I LOVE the sparkling sea,
    Its breath is life to me;
    The beckoning surges call me from afar.
    The breezes, sent before,
Will meet me on the shore,
Where Neptune waits to launch me in his car.

The Tritons blow their horns.
Aurora blushing scorns
To linger by the old man's bloodless side.
The ancient mariner
And first adventurer,—
"Away," he cries, "across the waters wide."

The word Æolus hears.
He hangs his sullen ears,
And, muttering thunders, smites the hollow cave.
The winds, the winds are out,
In revel and in rout,
To dance the Devil's dream upon the wave.

Oh, swifter than the steed,
Whose wings give double speed,

We bound from crest to crest along the main.
The foam is on our hair;
The spray is everywhere;
Our eyes are blinded with the briny rain.

'Tis now we touch the stars;
'Tis now we graze the bars;
My brain—it reels, my heart—it stops; Give o'er,
I cried, and swooned away.
I woke; the sunset lay,
Like heaven's light upon the farther shore.

The Sea-god's mighty hand
Was steering to the land.
"Look up," he said; and lo, a star serene,
More gracious than the light
Of morning, lit the night!
" Venus," he said, " our cynosure; thy queen."

This land, said I,—it seems
The Eden, that in dreams
I once descried when youth was in my heart.
I know it by those bells!
Oh, list! their rapture swells
More tuneful than Cecilia's purest art.

And o'er the lessening reach
Between us and the beach,
4

Melodorous fragrance wafted comes to me ;
As 'twere her honeyed breath,
Whose fond soul whispereth
Itself away in love's sweet ecstasy.

O love, I come to thee
Across life's stormy sea—
To thee and home, Earth's only paradise ;
Whose glory is thine eye,
Thy voice its melody,
Thy grace its flower and perfume.   Happy thrice,

Oh, thrice, thrice happy he
Whose youth is wed with thee !
My hope was there; fruition crowns my quest.
I tread that shore, and feel
Love's drowsy languor heal
The tempest's woes, and fill my heart with rest.

I would I were the sea,
And thou a mermaid free;
Its wealth untold, O love ! should be thy dower.
Couched in my being's deep,
The watches of thy sleep
Should be the ebbings of its tidal power.

There is a boundless sea,
God's blessed deity,
Awaits our life and all its love so dear
Thither our spirits glide,
To mingle with that tide,
And in it find their heaven's immortal sphere.

IN THE HAPPY SUMMER TIME.

PIRIT I seemed to be, on the air floating,
  Lost in a luminous sense of existence.
Noises of earth I heard, borne far and faintly,
    In the quiet Autumn time.

Slowly uplifting me, rising and falling,
  Wavered the aestuose tides of the air-sea.
Suddenly shrinking they fled. tempest-stricken,
    In the dreary Autumn time.

Hurled was I then with the snow-flakes and driven;
  Low on the moor laid, insensate and frozen,—
Laid like a clod, with the clods of the fallow,
    In the awful Winter time.

Still stood the Sun, for a day, in that valley
  Of shadow and death—for a day, and, relenting,
Turned, while the elements wept; and I dreamed then,
    In the woful Winter time.

Then all was night again.   Night of such darkness
  Only the dead know,—nor know it.   "Awake thou,"
Thundered a voice, whispered, sighed, and entreated,
    In the glad—in the sweet Spring time.

Breath of the icy North, northward returning,
　　Laden with languor and rapture and passion;
Boughs of the thorn-tree, with swollen buds laden,
　　In the Spring, in the fond Spring time.

Orchards, full-drifted with snow banks of apple-blooms;
　　Mould of all earthiness, wrought into beauty,
Thrilled into fragrance and flushed with the throbbings
　　Of glorious, green Spring time.

Started and thrilled all my soul, re-embodied
　　In numberless exquisite senses, a harp
Swept by great Pan,—by his fingers symphonic,
　　In the happy Summer time.

Trill of the lark from the morning-lit heavens,
　　Blue of the blue-bird and gold of the oriole,
Falling and flashing and splendoring together,
　　In the happy Summer time.

Heat of high noon, and the reapers reposing;
　　Honey-bees drowsing, as drunken with poppy;
Only the fly and the bumble-bee stirring,
　　In the happy Summer time.

Crash of the lightning, and pulse of the sleeping sea
　　Under the silent stars; moon-lighted lovers;
Dream-lands and fairy-lands; visions and voices,
　　In the happy Summer time.

Islands of palm-trees, fair, emerald islands,
　　Floating on azure in sunsets of topaz,—
Haunts of the South-wind that sleeps in their shadow,
　　　　In the happy Summer time.

Rest with me, love, on the bank where the South-wind,
　　Coursing the deep, flings the joy of its fountains,—
Their rapturous coolness again from its wings,
　　　　In the happy Summer time.

Rest with me here, on the sweet sod of Summer;
　　Weave, love, the silk-worm's web over and round us;
Pass with me thus to the Soul universal,
　　　　In the happy Summer time.

REMEMBRANCE.

THOU art a dream, my love, thou art a dream.
　　Ravished by time and distance from my
　　　　sight,
　　Thy absence turns the noontide into night;
And our fond loves, that were so living, seem
　　　The ghost of dead delight.

Thou art a voice, my love, thou art a voice
　　Lingering in a forever dying tone
That vibrates in the aching heart alone,
　　And all sweet sounds beside—a jangling noise,
　　　　　A pain, a grief, a groan.

Thou art a shadow, love, the shadow cast
　　Upon life's present moment by the thought
Of happiness that was, but now is not;
　　The memory impassionate of a past
　　　　　With passion over-fraught.

Thou art a sigh, my love, thou art a sigh;
　　The whispering zephyr, after that the rain
Of sobbing storms has ceased, and come again
　　The calm of star-light to the weeping sky,
　　　　　And on the troubled main.

Where art thou, dearest?   Where the happy spot,
  That feels the press of thy beloved feet?
What star or planet fair?   What field or street?
  Alas, where e'er it be, I know it not,
      Nor when our lips will meet!

But some day I shall clasp thee, on that shore
  Where neither mountains rise nor oceans roll;
Whose light and atmosphere will be thy soul;
  And thou the vision I shall there adore,
      Life's rest, reward and goal.

ODE IV, BOOK I. HORACE
TO LUCIUS SESTIUS.

SPRING'S glad succession and the western wind
Dissolve stern Winter and his ice-chains
break.
The ships, dry standing, leave the banks
behind,
Drawn down on groaning trucks to sea and lake.
No longer now the folded herds delight
In stalls of thatch, or tasteless husks desire.
The meads with hoar frost are no longer white;
And the rude swain ignores the blazing fire.
Now Cytherea leads her choiring bands,
The moon meridian looking from her seat.
The pleasing Graces with the nymphs join hands,
And strike the earth with ever changing feet;
While glowing Vulcan lights with thunder brands
The heavy forges where the Cyclops beat.
Now it becomes the shining head to wreathe
With the green myrtle, or the early flowers
That love to blossom on the mellow heath ;—
Now unto Faun to slay, in leafy bowers,
A lamb or kid, as with his wish agreeth.

Death, pale of cheek, invades with equal pace
The rich man's palace and the poor man's shed.
O Sestius opulent, life's little space
Forbids us enter on the hope ahead
Far reaching. Soon the night will press thee on,
And soon the fabled shades and cheerless hall
Plutonian. When thither you are gone,
No more to you the shaken dice will call,
As master of the merry realms of wine;—
No more fair Lycidas will you admire,
For whom each youth now burns with flame divine,—
For whom the virgins soon will feel love's warm desire.

ODE VII, BOOK I. HORACE.
TO MANATIUS PLANCUS.

OME Mytelene, or illustrious Rhodes,
Or Ephesus, or the high walls which stand
Warders of Corinth and her peaceful codes
Exposed to armed fleets on either hand;
Or Thebes the mother of the god of wine,
Or Thessaly renowned for Tempe's vale,
Or Delphi for Apollo's mystic shrine,—
Some these will praise; while others, in a tale
Of endless verse, all labor else forgone,
The city of chaste Pallas celebrate,
And with an olive bough their temples crown
From every spot her heroes consecrate.
In Juno's honor many a one will sing
Argos, the nurse of steeds of fiery eye;
Mycenae too, grown rich in treasuring
The yellow gold. Not Sparta, if she lie
In meek submission to her tyrant's will,
Has me so struck, nor I the campus love—
Fertile Larissa's, as the mountain rill,
Resounding Albunea's home; the grove
Tiburnian,—the craggy Anio, and

The orchards moist with running rivulets.
As oft from murky skies the South wind bland
Removes the clouds, nor constant showers begets,
Do thou remember, Plancus, even so,
Wisely to terminate with soothing wine
The toils of life, and thus its griefs forego;
Whether for thee the camps with standards shine,
Or thy umbrageous Tiber thee retain.
Tho' Teucer fled his sire and Salamis,
Yet with a poplar garland he was fain
To bind his temples, so the story is,
Wet with Lyæan wine, and thus to cheer
His weeping friends:—" Whithersoe'er, I say,
O boon companions and associates dear,
Fortune shall lead, thither we will away!
More gracious than a parent's is her care.
With Teucer's leadership and augury,
Of nothing must your fearless hearts despair,
Since truthfully Apollo promised me
Another Salamis upon the shore
Unknown. Ye braves, who oft with me before
Have suffered greater ills, with wine now banish sorrow.
Over the wide sea we shall journey on the morrow.

LIBERTY.

I.

 STOOD upon the shore of a wide sea
     Restlessly rolling.
Loud is thy plaint; what may its burden be?
     I said, condoling.

Is it remorse for those who, left to die,
     To the escheating,—
Thy multitudinous hands smothered their cry,
     Vainly entreating?

Or is it sorrow for the wreckage wrought;
     The storm compelling;
While, in thy depths so troubled and distraught,
     Thou wast rebelling?

For thou of old hast been a friend to man
     Blindly obeying
The law of force—but for some better plan
     Hoping and praying.

So, pausing, thou didst part to make a way
    For bondmen flying.
Turning again, lo, where the tyrant lay
    Engulfed and dying!

Mingling its own with thy mysterious light;
    Divinely beaming;
Faith's mystic planet traversing earth's night;
    A vision seeming

Of saints and seraphs, once the Holy Grail,
    Wondrous in story,
Across thy waters left its world-wide trail
    Of grace and glory.

And when the powers of light and darkness strove,—
    Truth with delusion,
And Freedom's Ark before the tempest drove,
    Of revolution,

Making no port,—less fearful of the forms
    Of thy commotion,
Hope launched it forth on thy protecting storms,
    Thou mighty Ocean.

And here uprising on thy wave-beat strand
    In strength and beauty,
And holding Hope's bright beacon in her hand,
    In grateful duty

She—Freedom—seaward turns, to thee. Her light
　　　Shall perish never,
Whilst thou below, in majesty and might,
　　　Rollest forever.

II.

Hail, holy Liberty;
Spouse of humanity;
Mother of equity;
　　Angel of light!
Blest be the city, on
Which thy fair eidolon
Beams when the day is gone,
　　Star of the night.

Lo, where thy exiles,
From hate and oppression, come
Seeking a hearth and home
　　Over the sea,—
Here, by Columbia's gate,
Thou dost in welcome wait,
Showing the high Estate
　　Founded by thee.

Wild was the wave when thou,
Guiding the pilgrim's prow,
Leddest thy chosen through
　　Darkness and deep.—

Wilder their fury, whose
Murderous madness chose
Faggots and fangs for those
   Whom thou didst keep.

Free and American
My fellow-countrymen,
Native or alien,
   They were our sires.
Born of their spirit,
The name we inherit—
The same let us merit,
   Redeemed by the fires

That lighted a nation
Its way to salvation,
Through red tribulation
   And Valley Forge;—
That woke the world's wonder
At chains rent asunder,
And slaves freed from under
   The curse and scourge.

III.

Amen; so may it be—
Freedom and equity
  Now and for aye.

Answer, thou swelling main;
Thunder thy glad refrain.
Echo it back again,
 River and bay.

Amen; amen again.
Peace and good will to men,—
 These are thy themes,
Saint of the battle-field;
Witness and martyr sealed;
First unto men revealed
 In songs and dreams.

Amen; so shall it be.
He who so patiently
 Suffereth wrong,—
By His eternal right
Thou shalt thy foes requite,
And in triumphant might
 Utter thy song.

PERCY BYSSHE SHELLEY.

INCARNATE voice of song, between
the soul
And her ideal thou, a god, dost
stand.
Sublime of height, that world to either pole—
Realm beyond realm opens before thee; and
The stars lie in the compass of thy hand.

And then, transcendent artist, on thy scroll,
In elemental characters of light
Thou dost portray thy vision, and unroll
The revelation to our human sight.
Look, mortal, look! It is Parnassus' hight

O minstrel eloquent! so may we learn
To listen and to love, that in the day
When we stand forth, each in his little turn,
The hymnings of the choirs seraphic may
Attune our hearts to their supernal lay.

' Tis so, that when, as Iris while she flies
   Trailing the solar splendors on the wrack,
Thy genius soars across its native skies,
   For it the morning stars, that sang, give back
   The music of the spheres along its track.

LILIAN ADELAIDE NEILSON.

HERE Nilus flows, great river of the gods,
   Past old Egypta's fanes;
Where lovers languish, and the lotus nods,
   And dreamy silence reigns;

Where in the youth-time of the Pharaohs
   Osiris walked the earth;
Where Art was born, and Architecture rose,
   And Science had her birth,—

There was the cradle of thy genius; there
   Thy wondrous lineage sprang.
Primeval demigods thy fathers were,
   And thee the poets sang,

From Homer down, in Helen, and that queen
   Whose life the flames up-swept;
And also in Cleopatra, I ween,
   Thy tragic pathos wept,

O child of rhapsody and passion,
   With whose poetic soul
Europa's storms and Afric's dazzling sun
   Were blended, in that role

Wherein we saw thee madly sighing, so
  As it were death to part;
Then lost in love's unutterable woe,
  And dead on Romeo's heart.—

Wherein thou wert fond Psyche, all aglow,
  Whose trembling heart beat fast;
And then divinest sorrow—" Romeo,
  " I come, I come at last."

Fair Star, when thou that zenith didst ascend
  Where genius shines alone,
The world below was proud to be thy friend,
  And make thy cause its own.

But when detraction's rank, invidious breath
  Thy lustrous name profaned,
Ephemeral as the planet's lunar wraith,
  Its fickle worship waned.

Yet still thou shinest, moving toward that Sphere
  Whose gates are never shut;
And where at last thy spirit will appear
  A seraph glorious.—But,

The generous sentiment and noble soul
  Of chivalry have fled
And, wrapped in pietism's mummy-roll,
  Sweet charity lies dead.

WESTCHESTER—IDYL.

OW Day departing, on the Western bound
Turns to salute her elder sister, Night.
That sullen hag, as the sweet Day looks
round.
From her black, wrinkled face all bathed in light
Flings back a thousand splendors;—e'en the ground
Whereon she walks with glory is bedight,
And she a beauty made who erst was born a fright.

Fair land of purple hills, rising afar,
Thou art my theme, however varying
The notes I touch.   Twilight and evening's star
Be only symphonies.   One song I sing.
Hymning thy praise, all other praises are
But echoes of thine own.   In the bright ring
Of thoughts, however chased, thou art the pearly thing.

Fair land of purple hills, rising afar,
Hight beyond hight, until their summits seem
Steps to the skies—whose Titan hands unbar
Those gates that stand, as in the seer's dream
The gates of Heaven stood, gloriously ajar
Upon thy bourne at sunset, when the gleam
Of blazing sapphires falls from the blest lights supreme?

When first I turned my restless feet to thee,
I came a weary wanderer forlorn.
Deceived of men, mocked of adversity,
Upon me dawned thy hope's auspicious morn.
For thou didst hope inspire : thy sympathy
Was a new life, healing the wounds of scorn—
The breast of Nature to the child of Nature born.

In the wild storm and in the whispering gale,
In every murmuring stream and singing bird,—
The crashing thunder and the echoing vale,
It was the voice of Nature that I heard.
Its eloquence did every sense assail ;
And every answering chord within me stirred
Could only silence keep, where language had no word.

Fair land, the guiding hand that led me on
To lay my soul an offering at thy shrine,
Now points remembrance back ; and like the swan,
Whose dying strains all dulcet notes combine,
My heart recalling joys forever gone,
And pausing on the verge of hope's decline,
Pours out its fond lament for "days of auld lang syne."

O Memory, thou ever constant friend,
How wondrous is thy life ! Change nor decay
Impairs thy youth ; while the dissolving end,
Which sweeps together men and moons away,

Is ever thy beginning;—as ascend
The stars of light at the dark death of day,
So of the dying present thou art born for aye.

My heart's Arcadian home, upon thy hills
How many pilgrims, weary unto sleep,
Have pitched their silent tents; life's feverish ills
The greater and the less, quenched in the deep,
Unbreaking slumber. Memory comes and tills
The sacred sod, whose wreathing ivies creep
Wet with the dewy tears that love and reverence weep.

But where the passionless, perchance more blest,
Had found in thee a grave, a cradle I:
For there my heart was born. As in their nest
The hatching brood, by hunger taught, do cry,—
So, to its nascent longing and unrest,
Love gave a voice. In vain did Nature try
To soothe me, fond old nurse, with her soft lullaby.

For I would not be soothed. Was the fault mine,
If fault there were, that not with blandishment,
O Cupid, thou arch playfellow divine,
Thy mother's lusty child would be content?
Kisses—they be love's only anodyne.
The fevering poison by thine arrows sent
Her lips alone can draw, and quell the bleeding rent.

With the sweet strain, whose theme is love's distress,
War's horrid turbulence discordant blends.
Tempest and calm, fury and tenderness,
No concord know, else hell and heaven were friends.
Yet slaughter dire and passion's caress
On Earth one picture make; one voice ascends,
The avenging cry in which the song of Eden ends.

God of our fathers, whose creative plan
Evolved this earthly stage, where crime and wo,
Masked in thy image,—so Thou madest man,—
In dreadful majesty stalk to and fro,
Thy purpose infinite we cannot scan,
Yet, finite as we are, too well we know
The tragedy is real, however grand the show.

From her blest station Mercy stands at gaze,
The more confounded while she looks again.
Nations in arms arrayed her sight amaze:
Amazement turns to stony horror, when
A carnival of lust amid the blaze
Of cities sacked she sees. Hell shudders then
Herself, while kings and popes cry, "Glory!" and "Amen!"

Fair Leyden, star of Freedom's rising state,
Fierce was the fight that gave thy arms renown.
Thy hands, all bleeding, wrenched the sword of hate
From tyranny, and threw Rome's idol down.

Thou—thou that harlot's thirst didst satiate
With gall, and blight the Spanish Gorgon's frown.
God's be the praise,—and thine the conquest and the crown.

Spirit of Liberty, thy home is found
In every heart that loves thy sacred name.
Thou hast no dwelling else.—The world around,
All climes and countries are to thee the same ;
But, where the dykes of Holland set a bound
To foes, whose whips thy soul could never tame,
There first, in Church and State, thy kingless kingdom came.

So I salute thee, Holland, in the lay
That chants the praises of my own fair land.
Ye stood together in that evil day
When English patriots felt the iron hand
Upon their necks.—Sailing up yonder bay,
Thy exiles came, while Plymouth's rocky strand
Welcomed with hoarse acclaim the Mayflower's pilgrim
        band.

And here, Westchester, on thy storied plains
Their sons, our fathers, fought. The outraged earth,
Whene'er oppression's cruel lust profanes
Her sacred husbandry, gives spiteful birth
To armed giants, where the vernal rains
Had wooed her smile. There is no soil so dearth,
But tyrants find how much its yield of men is worth.

Ye smiling vales, where Summer holds her seat
Beneath the blue expanse of skies serene,
And Bronx, all wound about her flowery feet,
Enamoured glides his grassy banks between,—
Ye happy vales, of solitude replete,
Where wealth, world-weary, hides within your green,
Umbrageous depths, how changed the present, peacefu
    scene.

When he, of all our liberties the sire,
From your advantage ground defied the foe,
Dark was the hour. All ready to expire,
The embers of his country's hope burned low.
But in the hero's heart there was a fire,
Where Freedom kindled, as her despots know,
The torch whose beams their light round the wide world do
    throw.

A wilderness before him, in his rear
Uprose disaster's visage frowning black.
But, smiling at defeat, he mocked at fear,
And, turning in his Northward march, struck back,
Dealing the hirelings ball for bullet, here
Where ye did see it. In the smoky wrack
Of war and night concealed, he kept his onward track.

O soil to their bright virtues consecrate,
Who made your pastures greener for their blood,

We tread, too little mindful of their fate
Who in the breach of battle fearless stood.
And still they stand, foundations in that state
Which lifts its Ararat above the flood
Of human destiny, a refuge fair and good.

When Chaos travailed in the mighty throes
That gave Creation birth, shoreless the deep,
Like a huge caul, did the young sphere enclose.
Again God spake, when, rolling heap on heap,
The waters fled.—And then thy hills uprose.
Yet still within its arms does the sea keep
Thee clasped, while on thy shore it sobs itself to sleep.

As when a lover, of his bride bereft,
All inconsolable his grief outpours;
And, holding fast the body that is left,
Takes to his heart the dust that he adores,—
So the fond sea, from thee asunder cleft,
All prostrate lies along the crumbling shores
Whose loss, in ceaseless sighs, its heaving breast deplores.

And I for thee, Arcadia, lament,
Like one who in his grief no solace knows.
The luckless wight, whose fortune all is spent,
His useless purse after his fortune throws.
But I my heart will keep till fate relent.
For he may smiling come, who weeping goes.
As, after darkness, light; and, after pain, repose.

FREDERICK III.

THOU flickering ray of pure and kindly light,
  Set in that royal socket whence the fire
  Of quenchless wars flashed forth upon th
    night
Of ages past, there is no happier sight
  Than peace enthroned beneath the golden tire
  That monarchs wear; there is no music, Sire,
Like that which soothes the crownèd hero's ears,
When, bending o'er his sleeping realm, he hears
  His dear name murmured in her constant dreams.
  Thy own name, Fritz, is that fond theme of themes.
The world, thou Prince of Pain, its empire lays
Of homage at thy feet, whose numbered days
  Propound again the fateful riddle,—why
  Despots who hate should live, whilst thou, who loves
    must die.

HARRY BRANDON.

ONE eventide, from solitude's despair
    A fugitive,—as the star-haunted sea
    From its own waste of waters ceaselessly
    To-landward yearns, and breaks in passion-
       ate prayer,
All night in-rolling and up-dashing there—
  Thus I, alone, and weary for the unrest
  That drives life's passion soul-ward in its quest,
Knelt on the heavenly threshold.   List! a cry,
  Bird-like and tremulous, and still more clear,—
  An echo from the unutterable sphere,
Nearer descending, filling all the sky,
Borne through the Gates of God.   Uplifted high
  They bid me pass where wingèd seraphim
  Responsive cry in the eternal hymn.

EDWARD MCGLYNN.

HRICE blessed priest of a thrice holy cause,
 Speak on ; a listening world is at thy feet.
 Cold is thy censer, but its offering meet
From thy impassioned, quenchless lips still
  draws
The breath that kindled it,—that, burning, awes
 The hand that fain would smother it. The Might
Invincible, whose other name is Right,
Still rules by thee : the child-devouring curse
That mocks the Christ and worships Moloch—worse
 Than Earth's first woe, the curse that now amain
 Wrings blood for sweat from human heart and brain,—
 This Herod-handed sin thou shalt retain,
And they that shrive it expiate Herod's crime,
Dying a death loathsome before its time.

THE MISERLY MILLIONAIRE.

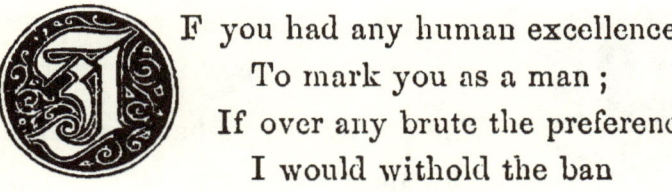 F you had any human excellence
      To mark you as a man ;
   If over any brute the preference,
      I would withold the ban

Of scorn your miserable soul deserves,
   If soul at all you have.
The villian, who his petty despot serves,
   Is not so poor a slave.

The sot, who welters in his drunkenness,
   Is less inebriate
Than you, whom your own sottish greediness
   Can never satiate.

Go, give some beggar-child a worn out cent,
   And, ere his eye can scan
The whole of it, bethink you and repent.
   God help you,—if He can.

SPRING.

E wintery storms and winds, farewell!
Spring has come with us to dwell.

The desolation ye have wrought,
She speedily will bring to naught,

Clothing the earth in verdure sweet,
Instead of frost and snow and sleet.

The fettered brook and ice-bound pond
Obey the magic of her wand.

The frightened birds come back again,
To chant the blessings of her reign.

Fragrance and beauty, life and song
Come, followers in her train along.

She breaths upon the frozen field,
And makes it like a mother yield.

Thus having blessed the grateful earth,
Sending us smiles where all was dearth,

She then entrusts the summer sun
To finish what she had begun.

For she must hie away, away,
Until a twelvemonth from to-day.

THE NEW AND VULGAR RICH.

 STOOD on the Fifth Avenue
   A-gazing at the crowd;
   And some were dressed so English,
   And some were dressed so loud,
I grew bewildered, wondering
What was what, and which was which,
A-gazing, on the Avenue,
At the new and vulgar rich.

And there I saw Miss Lillian Aire,
Whose fortune is untold,
As down the flashing thoroughfare
Her purple chariot rolled.
I used to know old Doctor Quack,
Her father, he was "sich";
And now they're on the Avenue,
With the rest of the vulgar rich.

He grew so rich—her father—
That at last it turned his head;
And then he fell a-thinking
He was growing poor instead.

He died of this delusion,
Not knowing which was which—
The Five Points, or the Avenue
Of the new and vulgar rich.

But what is this my eyes see,
So unlike the human kind!
One part goes prancing on before,
The other wags behind.
A woman or a Centaur?
I can't determine which,
A-stalking on the Avenue
Of the new and vulgar rich.

And yonder comes a gou-gou;
They seem as they would meet.
I never saw such flirting,
By daylight on the street.
His father was a Broadway Jew,
His mother was a witch;
And now he's on the Avenue,
With the new and vulgar rich.

I live in "Philadelphy,"
And I'm glad I have enough
Of other things to answer
For my lack of the cheap stuff,

That "gilds the straitened forehead"
Of the ambulating fool,
Who never knew his grandfather,
And never went to school.

I live in " Philadelphy,"
But in Boston was I born ;
Which tells you why I seem to speak,
With some degree of scorn.
To speak you fair, I'm in despair,
A-doubting which is which—
The Bay, or the Square, or the Thoroughfare
Of the new and vulgar rich.

MISS CLARA ST. CLAIR AND HER MIL-LIONAIRE.

ISS Clara St. Clair,
Of Louisberg Square,
Was growing to be a young lady.
Her mother had said
That Clara should wed
Prince Patrick Fitzpratrick O'Brady.
A widower and a millionaire;
A miserly, manifold prince and heir,
Whose heart was as hard as millstones *aire*,
She should, the lucky young lady.

But Clara St. Clair—
She did not despair,
Having eyes of her own for to see with;
And a will of her own,
And a till of her own,
To say who was the beau she'd agree with.
No Patrick Fitzpatrick O'Brady.
No widower and a millionaire;
No miserly, manifold prince and heir,
Whose heart was as hard as millstones *aire*,
Would she, the silly young lady.

Her father's pill-mills
And syrups and squills
Were posted and painted all over the hills.
Whence robes to astound,
And pearls by the pound,
And laces of diamonds her neck wound around.
And Patrick Fitzpatrick O'Brady,
The widower and a millionaire,—
A miserly, manifold prince and heir,
Whose heart was hard as millstones *aire*,
Made love to this regal young lady.

To divine Nahant,
As was now their wont,
The household removed for a change of air;
And every night,
By the moon's pale light,
A jewsharp played under her window there.
No Patrick Fitzpatrick O'Brady,
No widower and a millionaire,
But a generous, spendthrift, nobody's heir,
Whose heart was soft as a Bartlett pear,
Thus wooed this susceptible lady.

Miss Clara St. Clair,
Of Louisberg Square,

Was missing one morning that summer;
     And footprints around,
     Where she jumped to the ground,
Just fitted the shoes of a drummer.
No Patrick Fitzpatrick O'Brady;
No widower and a millionaire,
But a generous, spendthrift, nobody's heir,
Whose heart was soft as a Bartlett pear,
     Had wooed and had won this young lady.

     The prince took to horse,
     Ere bad should be worse,
And spied them just entering Salem by Lynn.
     "A challenge!" he cried.
     The drummer replied—
"I'll fight you with pistols, close up to the chin,
"Prince Patrick Fitzpatrick O'Brady!"
The miserly prince and millionaire,
And the generous spendthrift, who did not care—
Oh, who do you think their seconds were?
     The mother herself and the lady.

     "At his wooden head
     "Aim your cartridge lead,"
Miss Clara St. Clair to her lover had said.
     "His impudent face
     "Is made out of brass,"
Said her mother, "aim low at his heart instead,

"Prince Patrick Fitzpatrick O'Brady."
The widower and a millionaire,
And the brazen-faced, spendthrift, nobody's heir,
Whose hearts were a millstone and Bartlett pear,
    Thus fought for that charming young lady.

        "One, two—fire."   Bang, bang!
        Poor Clara she sprang,
And lay prone on the face of her drummer quite dead.
        When over them fell
        The other pell-mell,
And smashed her and mashed her as if he were lead.
"O Patrick Fitzpatrick O'Brady!
"Thou widower and a millionaire,
"Thy heart, as hard as millstones *aire*,
"Has 'mashed' me at last, and some to spare;
    "I'll marry you," groaned the young lady.

THE MESCAL OF MONTEZUMA,

OR THE GREAT KETTLE OF POPOCATAPETL.

OUNTAIN of Anahuac, sublimely grand,
　　O Popocatapetl,
Astride thy peak did Montezuma stand,
Holding a vessel in his mighty hand!
　　It was a kettle,
　　O Popocatapetl,
　　It was a kettle!

He had gone up, near as I can find out,
　　On Popocatapetl,
With all his Aztec lords and peon rout,
His cactus kingdom for to look about,
　　Confound the nettle
　　From Popocatapetl,—
　　Confound the nettle.—

And plight the rising sun his royal troth,
　　On Popocatapetl;—
The cactus king to take the cactus oath
Wet with a stunning draught of cactus broth
　　From out that kettle,
　　On Popocatapetl,—
　　From that great kettle

89

Ah, reader, didst thou never lave thy whistle,
  On Popocatapetl,
With mescal softer than the down of thistle,
And fierier than the scorpion's sting-y bristle,—
  That crawling nettle
  Of Popocatapetl,—
  That crawling nettle?

Then go to Mexico, and fearless quaff,
  On Popocatapetl,
The stuff that makes her tropic daughters laugh,
And soon will make you languish like a calf;
  And let it settle,
  On Popocatapetl,—
  And let it settle.

'Twas a volcano in those days of old,
  This Popocatapetl,
Adown whose sides the lava sometimes rolled;
Such was the youthful freshness, I am told,
  And fiery mettle
  Of Popocatapetl,—
  Of Po-po-cat-a-pet-l.

The king had sworn that on this great occasion,
  On Popocatapetl,
He would cook up, for the whole Aztec nation,
Mescal enough for its intoxication,

In that same kettle,
On Popocatapetl,—
In that great kettle.

And there with the hot cauldron he did wrestle,
On Popocatapetl,
Hung from his hand as 't were a kind of trestle.
"Ye gods," he cried, "I'll bet I'll drop this vessel,
"Ye gods, I'll bet I will,
"In Popocatapetl;
"Ye gods, I'll bet I will!"

And so with that he did; and the wide muzzle
Of Popocatapetl
That precious mescal all did gorge and guzzle.
How it did sputter, hiss and fizzle-fuzzle
In the red throttle
Of Popocatapotl,—
In that red throttle.

This was the last of Popocatapotl,—
Of Popocatapetl.
Take care! You sometimes never can tell what'll
Betide your own throat, from the uncorked bottle
Filled from that kettle
Of Popocatapetl,—
From that great kettle.

O Montezuma, mighty mescal man!
　　　O Popocatapetl,
That overlookest Ochopetlahuacan
And Iztaccihuatl!—Pronounce them if you can,—
　　　O big brass kettle
　　　Of Popocatapetl!
　　　O great Quetzalcoatl!

TOUNG TALOUNG.

AIL sacred brute! Thrice welcome to these
   shores,
Whereon the surges of Atlantic's main
Swept by the winds that heralded thy fame
And bore it hitherward, break ceaselessly,
Resounding in our unaccustomed ears
The voice of an adoring nation's cry,
As 'twere the noise of many waters. Hark,
"Toung, Toung Taloung, Taloung; Toung, Toung Taloung.'
Forth issuing from his shrine of beaten gold,
Lo, lo, he comes—Asia's incarnate Light!
His step all majesty, his mien all grace,
His eyes all calm, his face all mystery.
And hark again, the god-mad people's voice-
The thundering plaudits of a sea of souls:
" Toung, Toung Taloung, Taloung; Toung, Toung Taloung.'

Upon his throne Siam's imperial sire
Sits mute and melancholy. Round his head,
His murky brows besplendoring, a zone
Of yellow gold girdles a world of thought.
Surmounted with a regal diadem,
And waxing heavy and still heavier,

So droops the sable sunflower, when the light,
Toward which it fondly turns, goes out in night.

Lift up thy head, O King!   Thy setting sun,
Taking the westward way of Empire's star,
Rises effulgent on a race of kings,—
A sovereign people.   Welcome, Toung Taloung;
And may thy advent be the dawning morn
Of a new era, on the western world;—
The wisdom of the Orient, the art—
The artless art of living to enjoy
Life's best, supremest gift—even itself.
Bring with thee, then, the light of tropic skies;
The spirit of an Asian afternoon;
The *dolce far niente* of a day
Whose gladness blooms in lily flowers, and lays
The hush of peace upon the sons of men
And meekness born of peace.

                    And Siam, peace—
Peace to thy fears, till Buddha re-appear
Lighting the darkness of thy soul's eclipse,
Wherein strange shapes appall thee; as the wrath
Of all the gods were leveled at thy sin,
Which flood and famine yet may expiate.
Our transport pleads for thee a first offense,
And thy great sorrow writes it down the last—
Forevermore the last.

Hail, Toung Taloung!
Thou art our wonder, and our children's joy.
Their little hands shall reach to touch thee, while
Thy amiable eyes bespeak their love.
Then, drawing back in counterfeited fear,
Their merry laugh shall echo in thy soul.
" Taloung, Taloung!"—their childish lips shall cry ,
And thy deep-voicèd bellow answer them :
" I am Taloung—Taloung the Worshipful.
" The Earth-god brought me forth ; upon my brow
" The Fire-god set his seal ; the Water-god
" Upheld me, while the Wind-god wafted me
"O.'er many seas,—Taloung the Worshipful."

MY LOVER TRUE.

Y lover true a shepherd is,
    Of lowly shepherds born.
  His cradle was the mountain glen;
    His cry the echoing horn.
The lambs and kids his playmates were;
  The fold his nursery.
I care not what the world says;
  He is all the world to me.

The mountain's hight is on his brow;
  The distance in his eye.
He climbs to meet the morning star,
  And fades against the sky.
The world blow soils not his soul
  With its fair falsity.
I care not what the world says;
  He is all the world to me.

And I am all the world to him,—
  It's compass, mete and bound,
Whose heart, to overflowing,
  I fill with joy profound.

His style is nature's majesty;
  His manner fond and free.
He cares not what the world says;
  And he's all he world to me.

Oh, would you woo my shepherd true
  To leave his native wild,
And in your school of folly
  Become a wiser child?
To laugh or weep, as loveless lips
  Shall pipe the changing key?—
To care for what the world says,
  Who is all the world to me?

Then there you'll find the happy heart
  To laugh you all to scorn—
My laughter-loving shepherd,
  Of lowly shepherds born.
And here you'll find the heavy heart
  To weep indeed, when he
Shall care for what the world says,
  Who is all the world to me.

LOVE'S ANCHORITE.

ERE my beloved dwelt. Knocking, I cried:
    Open to me, O thou beloved one.
  And hark,—" Who cometh there," her voice
    replied,
  "My love, or one unknown?"

Then, my beloved answering, I prayed:
  'Tis I, 'tis I; arise, open to me.
"Alack, O friend, there is not room," she said,
  " Within for ' me ' and thee."

Stricken and mute, my heart within me fell;
  And, turning, to the wilderness I fled;
Communing with myself:—It would be well
  For thee, if thou wert dead.

In this unknowingly I spake a truth;
  And wandered weary and ahungered there.
As they in whose afflicted souls the ruth
  Of sin is changed to prayer.

Long days and weary nights I passed, the while,
  Upon my grief inflicting tortures vain.
There was no other pang could this beguile.
  Then I returned again.

Here my beloved dwelt.   Knocking, I cried:
   Open to me, O thou beloved one.
"Who cometh there,"—'twas the same voice
     replied,
   "My love, or one unknown?"

Too worn and weary for myself to sue,
   'Tis thou, 'tis *thou*, I cried in ecstacy.
And she:—"Come in, thou welcome love and true;
   I, too, am lost in thee."

THE POET AND THE BIRD.

ARK,—I hear the red-breast calling,
   In the wintry morn ;
While the frozen tears are falling
   From the skies forlorn.
Nature still looks back in sorrow :
   All my heart is sad.
Hope is prodigal to borrow,   .
   And the bird is glad.

Robin, would thou hadst my reason—
   I thy happy song.
Love and life are out of season,
   And regret is long.
Winter's frost is but external :
   Life and youth must part ;—
Age involve and freeze the vernal
   Passions of the heart.

Endeth here the hymn of sadness,
   Disappointment, ruth ?
Listen to the poet's madness :—
   In it there is truth,—

As the bird of passage, flying,
  Soars to sunnier skies,
Love shall plume his pinions, dying,
  And divinely rise
To another life, whose portal
Is the gate of the immortal
  Spirit's Paradise.

FOREVER AND FOREVER.

T was not with an idle love,
My lost one, that I loved thee.
The spirit of the gods above
Was in the spell that moved me.

I would have borne thee on my heart
Forever and forever;
Life of my life, from whom to part
Had been that life to sever.

And now I live, I know not why,
Wounded, bereft, unhoping.
The light has faded from the sky;
I wander blindly groping.

Ah, night whose day was so divine!
Ah, earth that once was heaven!
Ah, pain that knows no anodyne!
The weary years are seven,

Since last I slept the happy sleep
Whose pillow was thy breast, love;
Not dreaming that these eyes would weep,
With sight of thee unblest, love.

But deep within the lees of life
There is nepenthe ; drink again.
Unresting from the toil and strife,
Forego the hope of happier men.

Nor is the lost one wholly lost,
Who leaves a ghost to haunt the years
With love's true image ; though the cost
Be life wept out in tears.

"NO."

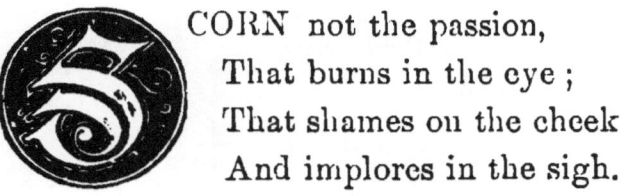

SCORN not the passion,
   That burns in the eye;
   That shames on the cheek,
   And implores in the sigh.

Love kindles the fire
That flushes the snow
Above with red streams
From the Hecla below.

Desire newly born
For life gasps; its breath
Is drawn in the sigh,
Whose suppression were death.

Oh, give back the sigh!
And, soft as the beam
Of morningtide, lay
The delirious dream

Consuming the orbs
That worship and weep.
What tears thou wilt shed,
If despair give them sleep!

Then, then thou wilt sigh,
When sighs will be sobs,
And pallor succeed
To the heart's stifled throbs—

"Come back; I loved thee;
"Forgive that I said."
Peace, peace; get thee gone,
Vex not, mock not the dead.

"Come back, my darling!
"Come back to be wed."
Hence, hence, where the feet
Of Heaven's angels tread.

THE AUTUMN FLIGHT.

THE wizard Year has laid his wand
    On Summer's sunny skies,
      And changed the green of fruit and frond
        To Autumn's scarlet dyes.
Of morning's chill upon the lea,
    And evening's dewy cloud
The hours are weaving silently
    Her white and frosty shroud.

The foes that filled her gentle ear
    With thunderous alarms,
Have grounded each his flashing spear,
    And rest upon their arms.
The blazon of their fiery wrath
    Hushed in the sad repose
Of Summer, on her couch of death,
    Still o'er the landscape glows.

Oh, wild will be the requiems,
    Tempestuous the dole,
When round her wintry grave their hymns
    Are chanted for her soul!

Then come, my heart, oh, come with me,
  Before that dismal night
O'ertakes the fields so fair to see,
  And leaves them ghostly white!

Ah, wherefore wouldst thou linger?
  To a deserted shore
The way-marks point their finger;
  And through the parlor-door
No music warbles from the band;
  The birds themselves have flown;
The billows, moaning on the strand,
  But leave thee more alone.

The stars look down as fixed and calm,
  Where thronging footsteps pass;
And flowers exhale as sweet a balm
  Beneath their skies of glass.
The charm of Autumn in the air,
  The languorous Indian noon
Will find thee in thy musings there,—
  Forsake thee, here, as soon.

Then come, my heart, oh, come with me,
  Before that dismal night
Descends upon the land and sea,
  And leaves them ghostly white!

I hear a voice that bids me so.
  My love, and is it thou?
I lost thee in the long ago;
  If I should find thee now!

No grasses grow along these ways,
  No blossoms wild and sweet;
No billows break in foamy sprays
  Round my advancing feet.
Yet here I kneel to kiss the pave
  My own love's feet have trod,
And left it laughing like the wave,
  And greener than the sod.

I passed along; I seemed alone;
  Nor face saw I, nor form.
And here the autumnal summer shone
  As dreamy and as warm.
When, soft, a voice that made me start,
  And kisses on my eyes!
My love, my love against my heart—
  My love and paradise!

And have I found thee, then, my love?
  Kisses were all his word.
Only his silent lips above
  My own fond lips were stirred.

Till, " Come, my own; oh, come with me,"
 He said, " before life's night
"O'ertakes the fields so fair to see,
 " And leaves them ghostly white! "

FJELDA.

HERE is a lake, a fond enchanting spot,
A favorite of Nature, who with skill
Has set it, like a diamond, within
A bed of living emerald; and when
Its crystal depth gives back the rainbow's hues,
Or yet, by night, the galaxy of heaven,
Behold thou there the signet-ring of God.
Its banks are eloquent, tradition-voiced,
Of one who trod their slopes, in beauty's form,
As 't were an angel's, cast, and gathered there
The pure, sweet violets, that, envying, saw
In her blue eyes a lovelier brilliancy.
And, laughing there upon the brink, she dipped,
Her fairy feet in the white, feathery foam,
While childhood broke for her its golden days,
And bathed her being in a flood of joy.
Do thou tread lightly, if it be that there
Thy feet shall wander and thine eyes behold.
The hoar old woods, that cast their shadows down,
And hasten night's approach to their retreats,
Are gnarled, and bent with age, and unto me
There's less of beauty than religion there.

The aged oaks twine their protecting arms
Over a crooked pathway magical
To lead you far within the leafy bowers,
Until you come upon a purling stream,
Spanned by a time-worn arch, throwing its spray
Over the mossy banks, with, here and there,
A recess garlanded with trailing flowers—
The first born blossoms of the early spring.

Morning, on heavenly wings, from her dark couch
Majestic rose, her loosèd locks of gold
The eastern sky bestrewing. From the world
Quiet of labors, sunk in sweet repose,
She gently drew the draperies of night.
Her yellow radiance like a blessing falls
Upon the hill, the vale, the wood, the lake,
Which, in the glory tranced, seem worshipping,
Rapt, in the presence of the king of day.
Just as the priest, in dazzling robes arrayed,
Forth from the vaulted sanctuary speaks
A benediction upon the throng
That, kneeling there in adoration, bow
Before the Lord of light and King of kings.
And as even there, sometimes, a thought profane
Silently, quickly steals across the soul,
Marring devotion's hush and holy hour,
So, from an alcove of embowering trees,

Rippling the bosom of the lake that seems
A sea of molten silver, in the glow
Of the fair morning splendor reveling
Upon it, swiftly glides a light canoe,
Obedient to a Northern maiden's will.
She is Fjelda, whom the outward world,
So full of light and life and love and joy,
Mocks, and impels from misery to death.
Bold and still bolder grow the liquid depths
Below the prow of the young princess' bark,
Speeding like a sprung arrow to its mark,
Until they sink where, dark and fathomless,
Their green abyss hides in mysterious caves.
Just now a zephyr, playing balmy sweet,
Fresh from the pure lips of the infant day,
Caresses her wan cheek, and cools her brow,
And kindly lifts therefrom the flowing tress
Silken and sunny as the white swan's wing.
"Great Odin, take thy child."—Fjelda prays,—
"Spirit of good, to whom my people bow.
"They call me mad, because I once did love;
"They call me evil, for that once to me
"A hope there was, a goddess had behooved,
"Charming the future to reality.—
"Now, hope-forsaken, love has turned to hate;
"And I am weary of the life that pours

"Across my spirit's harp-strings desolate,
"The harmonies my loathing soul abhors.
"Just as the mother lays her first-born down,
"To quiet sleep and dreams, in fondest trust,
"So, in this birchen cradle, let me drown—
"Ashes to ashes give, and dust to dust.
"But me—from the cold deep, oh! let me rise
"To thee, Allfather, and Valhalla's skies."
She spoke ; and, with her weapon, in the side
Of the frail boat she makes the fatal wound.
Swiftly within the serpent waters glide,
And lick and creep her prostrate form around;
And in her ears hiss a strange, awful sound—
Lullaby to her long and breathless sleep,—
Whisperings of spirits from a vaster deep,
Whose unseen hands bear to its unknown bed
The precious casket of the life—the clay,
Soon to be one among earth's countless dead,
And pass, like them, from memory away.
Pale and yet paler fades the hateful light;
Deeper and darker grows the friendly night,
Until the soul, expelled her laboring breast,
Enters Valhalla and Valhalla's rest.

8

THE MAID OF ROME.

I.

HE towers of Rome rise tall and fair
In the Italian sunset's glow;
The bells of Rome chime on the air,
Ringing, swinging, to and fro;
Calling to the place of prayer
Hearts to be beguiled of care,
Hearts whose burden of despair
Is of all the heaviest one.
From his torch the king of day,
Departing, flings a lingering ray
Of salutation to the queen
Who rises on his late demsne,
Luna of the Golden Horn—
Luna, queen of heaven born,
She, before another morn,
Will have passed in regal state
To her empire's western gate;
And before her majesty
Every star must veiled be;
Proving thus its fealty
To her high command;

114

Save indeed the noble few
Of her royal retinue,.
Gallant subjects, tried and true,
Men of her right hand ;
Princes, that have ever shone
Nearest to their sovereign's throne,—
Lords of empires all their own,
Realms that lie beyond the Sun.

II.

Like a dirge the holy sound
Falls upon the startled ear
Of the guilty captive bound
In his lonely dungeon near—
Echo of his ghostly fear.
For to him it is a knell,
And it speaks to him of hell,
Rousing fears he fain would quell.
For when chimes again shall call,
And the sacred shadows fall
On St. Angel's prison wall,
Where will be the prisoner then?
Ask the priest that shrives his soul,
Ask the prophet's flying scroll,
Ask the winds, or ask the sea,
Ask ye them, but ask not me ;
For of me ye ask in vain.

III.

Borne afar the hallowed strain
Reaches to the couch of pain,
Where the saint and sufferer
Feels the touch of death.
Monitor of hope and joy,
Soothing, sweet, without alloy;
From his God a whisperer,
Like a seraph's breath,
It will waft his spirit on
When with earthly trials done,
When life's victory be won,
To the heavenly rest.

IV.

In the dim, religious aisle
Penitents are bowed in prayer.
Through St. Peter's massive pile
Miserere's plaintive air
Soft re-echoes, where the while
Curving arch and column rare
Throw fantastic, spectral shades;
And the Virgin Mother's smile
Leaves a benediction there,
And the fainting suppliant aids.

Weary souls, believing pray—
Low on the cold pavement kneel.
What proud pharisee shall say
Ye no heaven-sent sorrow feel!
What presuming scribe declare
Your beads a mockery and snare,
Or your burden of emotion
But the semblance of devotion!
They that pray are they that feel
What speaking lips reveal.
Prayer is not the eloquence
That appealeth to the sense,—
Not the rounded utterance
Of a pious form;
But the language of the soul;
Of its voiceful speech the whole;
As the sea, whose beating roll,
Pulsing to the tidal power
Of the moon's meridian hour,
Sounds along the shore;
Or, as when the heaving swell,
Driven before the tempest's hell,
All its mighty thunderings tell
Of the distant storm;
And when winds have spent their force,
Surges then in accents hoarse,

Full of pity and remorse,
O'er the stranded sailor's corse
Grieving, wail and roar.

V.

There before the holy shrine
Of the holier Babe Divine,
While devotion pours its tide
Through the arches high and wide;—
Tide of peace whose heavenly flow
Soothes all sorrow, drowns all woe,
For the soul whose faith can rise
On the ascending symphonies,—
For the sinner who can hear
That unto the outward ear
Which the priestly lips proclaim—
Pardon in the Holy Name;—
Prostrate there a heart of sighs
In its dark profundities,
Like the sea beneath the reef
Of Scylla, rages with its grief.
Could its outward voice be heard,
Not a tongue of flesh were there,
Acolyte and monk and prior,
Priest and bishop, lord and 'squire,
Congregation all and choir,—

Not an echoing vault on high,
Where the columns meet the sky,
But would give an answering cry ;
By its piteous anguish stirred,
By the pathos of its prayer.

VI.

' Tis not manhood wrestles so
With the devil of its woe.
' Tis not he, whose iron will,
Taught by a long life of sin
How to hush the tongues within,
Can command them, " Peace, be still."—
Not the soul that, forced to fly
Itself before the dreadful cry
Of guilt, when o'er its prey it gloats,
Is fain to choke the noisy throats
Cerberian with the miry soil
That paves Perdition. Vain the foil.
But ' tis tender girlhood there,
In that agony of prayer ;
Gentle as the gentle fawn,
Modest as the blushing dawn,
And when yonder moon was young,
Pure as the supernal light
From the torches of the night
Through the azure spaces flung ;

Innocent as the white lawn
Round her girlish temples drawn
When, in confirmation's hour
Kneeling at the throne of grace,
Tears for Christ bedewed her face,
Holy hands being laid thereon
For the Spirit's benison ;
Sacrament of ghostly power.
Now the vulture of remorse
Preys upon the tortured corse
Of her maiden purity
With a dire rapacity.
Such the ghouls that upward flit,
When funereal lights are lit ;
To sepulchral banquets sped—
Fiends that fatten on the dead.

VII.

The pealing blasts no longer blow ;
A thousand echoing pipes are still.
The tuneful strains no longer flow,—
The tuneful, tearful strains that fill
The "Miserere" ; and has ceased
The voice of mediating priest.
The aisles are vacant ; and once more
The sacred sanctuary door

Is closed upon the Jesu's ghost,
Incarnate of the holy host.
One worshipper doth there remain,—
She that in the supremest pain
Of spirit travailed. Now her throes
Are ended—ended all her woes.
Before the altar of that place
Where Mary reigns the queen of grace,
Her form upon the floor of stone
Extended lies ;—the soul has flown.
The Virgin Mother saw the grief
That wrestled with high heaven there
In all the potency of prayer,
Like Jacob when he fought amain
The Angel on Penuel's plain,
And gave the penitent relief.
Descending from her starry throne,
Above, around her presence shone,
And lighted up her mystic shrine
With mercy's radiance divine.
Upon the sufferer's heart the spell
Of Mary's love benignant fell,
And lifted thence the infernal pall
That sin had wrapt her soul withal—
The infernal pall of hell and death.
As when the dazzling morning light

Breaks on the valley where the night
Has left its dank and poisonous breath,
The miasmatic vapors rise,
And the pure lake reflects the skies.

VIII.

While thus the ecstacy of peace
Fills every sense with sweet surcease
Of sorrow and of agony;
And the sore spirit knows its wound
The heavenly healing to have found
Of Christ's forgiving sympathy,
While thus, lo! at that shrine of tears
The blessed face itself. appears,—
Vision of beatific love,
And like a winged seraph moves
Before the suppliant, and proves
Its presence by a voice, and kiss,
Foretaste of the eternal bliss.
Then all unconsciously, as when
The sleeper wakes and sleeps again,
This watcher at the gate of heaven
Sinks 'neath the rapt oblivion
Which, cast from Mary's blessed glances,
Her sight and sense and soul entrances;

Until her limbs forget they kneel,
Until her lips forego their voice,
Until her brain begins to reel,
Until her senses cease to feel,
Until of life she has no choice;
Until she sinks, faints, falls,—until
Her pulse and heart and life are still.

IX.

As when the burning orb of day,
Ascending high and ever higher,
Shining with an intenser ray
Upon some flickering hearth-stone fire,
Quenches in its own heat the spark,
And leaves the embers cold and dark:
So Mary's glorious mother soul
Drew that sad life unto her own;
And left the unblest half of its whole
Dead, on the consecrated stone.

THE WRECK.

TWILL be a fearful night.
Across the deep,
Pitiless in their flight,
The wild winds sweep.
The billows, flinging high
Incense of spray,
Invoke the answering sky.
The murky wrack,
As ' twere a cerement
Of spectral shrouds
Woven of clouds,
Comes up the firmament.
The last, cold ray
Of a November day
Fades fast, and dies away.
Upon the track
Of their affrighted prey the sea-hounds growl;
As when the pack,
Chasing the fugitive, do yell and bay.
Nor would they pause, if so it were to be
The safety of a freighted argosy
And all on board, for whom the prayers and fears
Of wives and loved ones agonize in tears.

Across the wave
No beacon gleams,
To warn the sailor of an unknown grave;
To cheer, to guide and save,
No star-light beams;
While in the gloam,
Like fasted wolves that scent
The night-belated wanderer from the fold,
And tell unto the winds their fierce desires
In many a long-drawn howl;—
Or ghouls that, ill-content,
Swarm up from hell to vex the dead man's mould
With midnight carnivals, while nether fires
Purge the unshriven soul,
Lashed into foam,
The furious waters fiendish revels hold,
Hungry for spoil, mad for the writhing prey—
For manhood brave and beauty fair as day,
And all the wealth of gems and diamonds
And purple robes and tapestries, that comes
From Asia's treasuries and Persia's looms,—
These for the walls
Of palace halls,
Or for the regal feet of peers to press;—
Those, haughty forms imperial to caress—
Patrician youth and stately Saxon blondes;

And those in many a queenly tress to shine,
Or deck a lovely arm of mould divine—
An arm that Phidias might in vain contest,
Of so unwonted beauty 'twere possessed ;
Or stud a lovelier bosom white as snow—
Save that cerulean veins their coursings show—
In which the Graces seem yet more to vie ;
Where Love in nuptial slumbers fain would lie,
A captive to its charms and downiness,
A votary at that shrine of sweet redress—
The due reward of honor's chivalry.
But Ocean has the right to ask her own ;
Within whose womb grew the pure pearly stone,
And from whose breast distilled the gentle rains
That nourish, on the far-off Orient plains,
The fruitful flocks
Of silken locks,
Which the rustic shepherds to the brookside bring,
When Summer weaves her garlands for - the new made
      grave of Spring.
And if the jewel, whose exhaustless light
Plays round the brow empowered with regal might,
Has from the brighter sun its brilliancy,
Yet is it next of kin, O sea, to thee !
Alas, for the fell stroke !
Alas, for all the strength of bolted oak,

And all the hidden strength of wroughten ropes,
And wo to human hopes!
The ship that bears her burden to the west,—
Her winding sheet will be the billow's crest;
Her grave, the sunken reef; her funeral dirge,
The full deep bass of the storm-troubled surge.
Her bulk of costly draperies will be
A mocking pall for the humanity
Sleeping below, upon its coral bed,
Till immortality shall call the dead,
And clothe the skeleton whose dreamless head
Were ghastlier for the lapidary's skill
Sunk in the sockets eyes were wont to fill,—
Piercing the dark of deep, mysterious caves,
Whose floors the wealth of all the Orient paves.
O life, the lips that will expire to-night!—
The visions that will vanish, fond and bright!
O death, the forms thy cold embrace will chill,
Which now the blushing crimson loves to thrill!
How will thy ghostly finger lift that veil
Before whose revelation strong men quail!

Awake, bewildered dreamer, from the sleep
In which thy tearless eyelids fain would weep.—
Rouse from the horror of the imagery
That checks thy breath and makes thy senses shiver,
Intenser than the last reality,

The weird foreboding of the Stygian river.
Wipe from thy brow the clammy dews distilled
By racking fancies that thy brain have filled.
Arise, stern Fate is calling unto thee;
Awful her wings brook the nocturnal sea,
As round thy vessel, like a bird of prey,
Wheeling her flight she croaks her dismal lay.
The echo lingers in the winds, that shriek
Like spirits lost, striving in vain to wreak
Their vengeance on the maddened waves that sweep
Tumultuous the bosom of the deep.
Lo, here IT comes—
Thy Destiny!
Nor question why.
Trust thou in God.
His potent rod,
If so He will,
The mighty elements can still.
What if thy last long hour be near?
Gird up thy loins,—not, like a slave,
Crouch down with fear.
From it thou mayest not fly;
Then wherefore shouldest have
Such dread to die?
Weakling! canst thou disarm
The fury of the storm?

Or, when the deathly waves thy limbs shall clasp,
How canst thou, mortal, break their subtle grasp?
Alas, for thee! for thou shalt know
How much of terror and of wo
A single moment can inspire,
And prophesy unutterable;
When, from his paradise of dreams
Diffuse of morning's emerald beams,
Sleep startles at the roar
Of breakers on a desert shore,—
Ocean's reveille drums,
Calling to conflict dire;
To conflict with a foe
Invulnerable,
Unmerciful,
Insatiable.
The long ship staggering strikes,
With reeling shocks,
Upon the rocks.
The timbers stout and iron spikes,
Unequal to the strains
Of the gigantic giantess
Groaning in labor's pains,
Heaving in mortal throes,
Writhe and complain;
Strong to endure on the tempestuous main

9

Against the sea alone;
Weak to resist the bowlder's stunning blows
And the reef-covered strand
With many a carcass strown—
Oak-ribbed and bleaching on the sand.
Once noble hulls were they
Spurning the land,
Reveling in storm and spray.
Ah, what a sense of misery is here,
The ordeal of despair!
How blanched, how wild with dumb dismay appear
Its victims cowering there,
Pressing with weary feet the frozen deck!
O heaven, is this their recompense who yearn
To fill brimful of happiness
Their life's deceptive urn?
On that eventful morn,
How throbbing hearts, how faltering accents told
Of loves and friendships weightier than gold!
How doubt shrank back! How faith soared high and
    bright!
How false to hope ambition gave its plight!
How loving lips wooed loving lips again!
How ties of birth bound dear ones closer, when
Forth from her pier the heavy ship swung out,
And spread her wings to many a farewell shout!

O ye forlorn!
O wretched born!
O ye by visions of sweet home to-night
Tortured and worn!
Not long have ye to wait
To pass the crystal gate
That closes aye on earth's last agonies;—
Not long to abide
The final summons death delivers wreck.
Lo, changed in likeness to the tide,
The Spectre comes to claim his bride!
How lavishly he laves her side!
How passionate upon her breast
He throws his quivering form!
And look! a three-fold breaker now,
Towering amain above the prow,
Of might invincible possessed—
Terror wrought into storm!
From stem to stern the sickening tremor flies.
Dying the monster lifts herself in air,—
'Tis the last effort;—down, to fragments down,
Crashing, she settles on the rocky bed.
And trembling hope forevermore has flown;
And oh, for aye the fond good-bye is said;
And heaven has heard the last, beseeching prayer.
And now the embrace, the cry, the awful leap,
The struggle brief, the silence, and the sleep.